HOW TO BE A
Super Villain

A colorful and fun children's picture book; entertaining bedtime story

Rachel Yu

rachelbookcorner.com

www.rachelbookcorner.com

ISBN-10: 1463739168
ISBN-13: 978-1463739164

Printed in the United States of America.

For Mom, Dad, Eric, and Bear

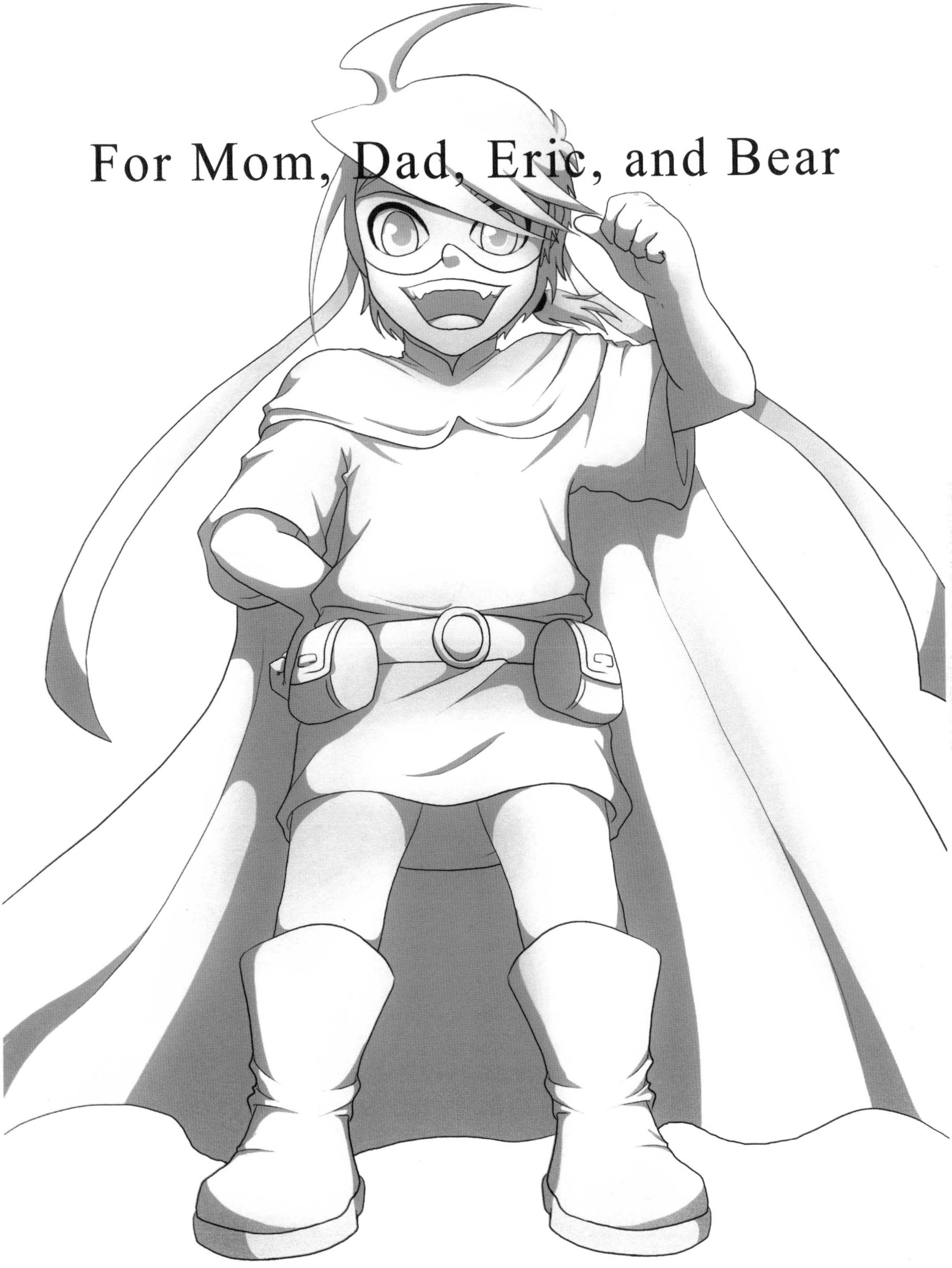

"Hello there! Welcome, please come in! I am Supreme Master of Awesomeness, and today I will teach you how to be a Super Villain."

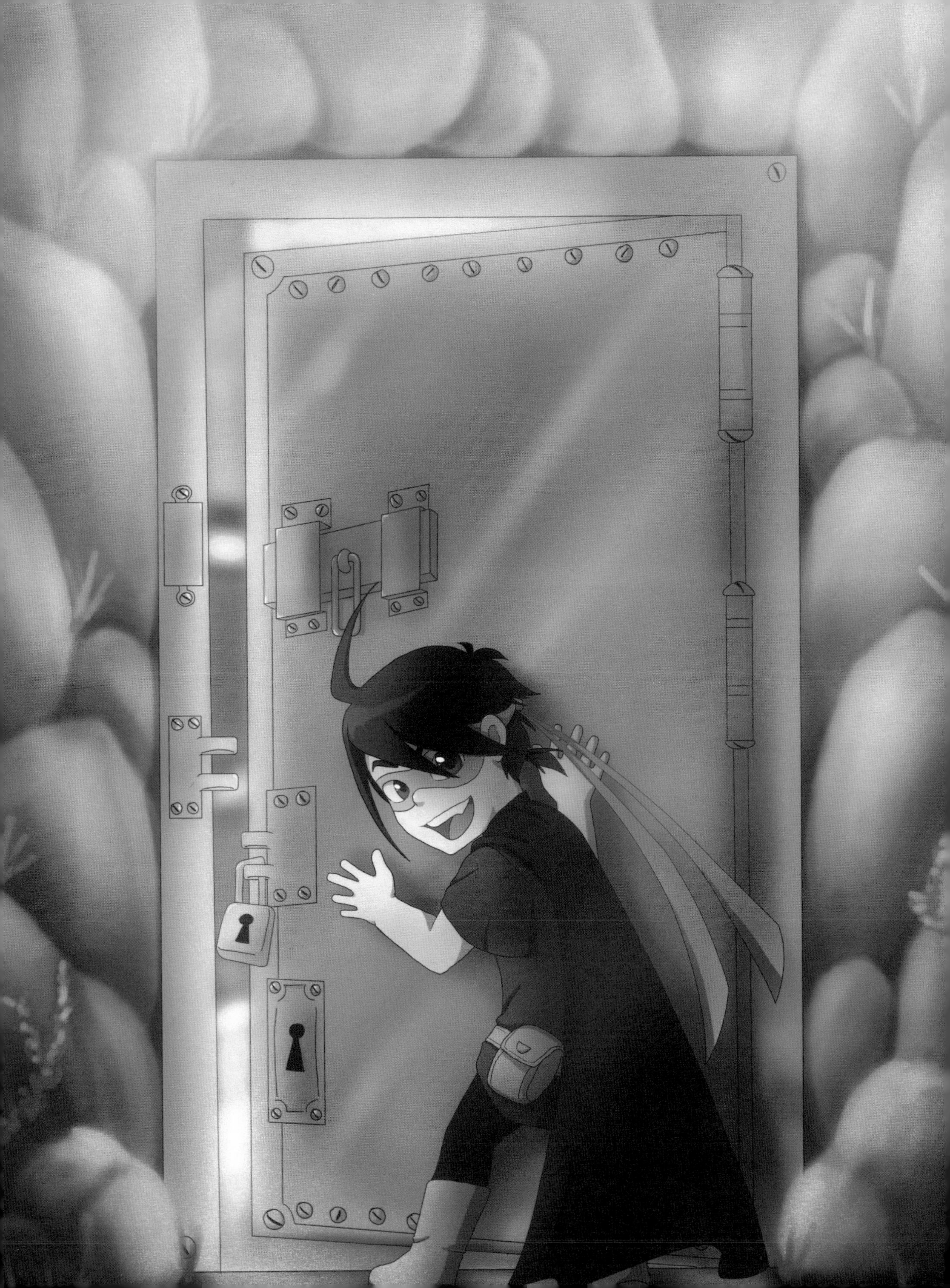

"Now, the first step in being a Super Villain, is to have a tricked out, super cool and super secret hideout. This is my Lair of Awesome! It's pretty neat for an old cave, right?"

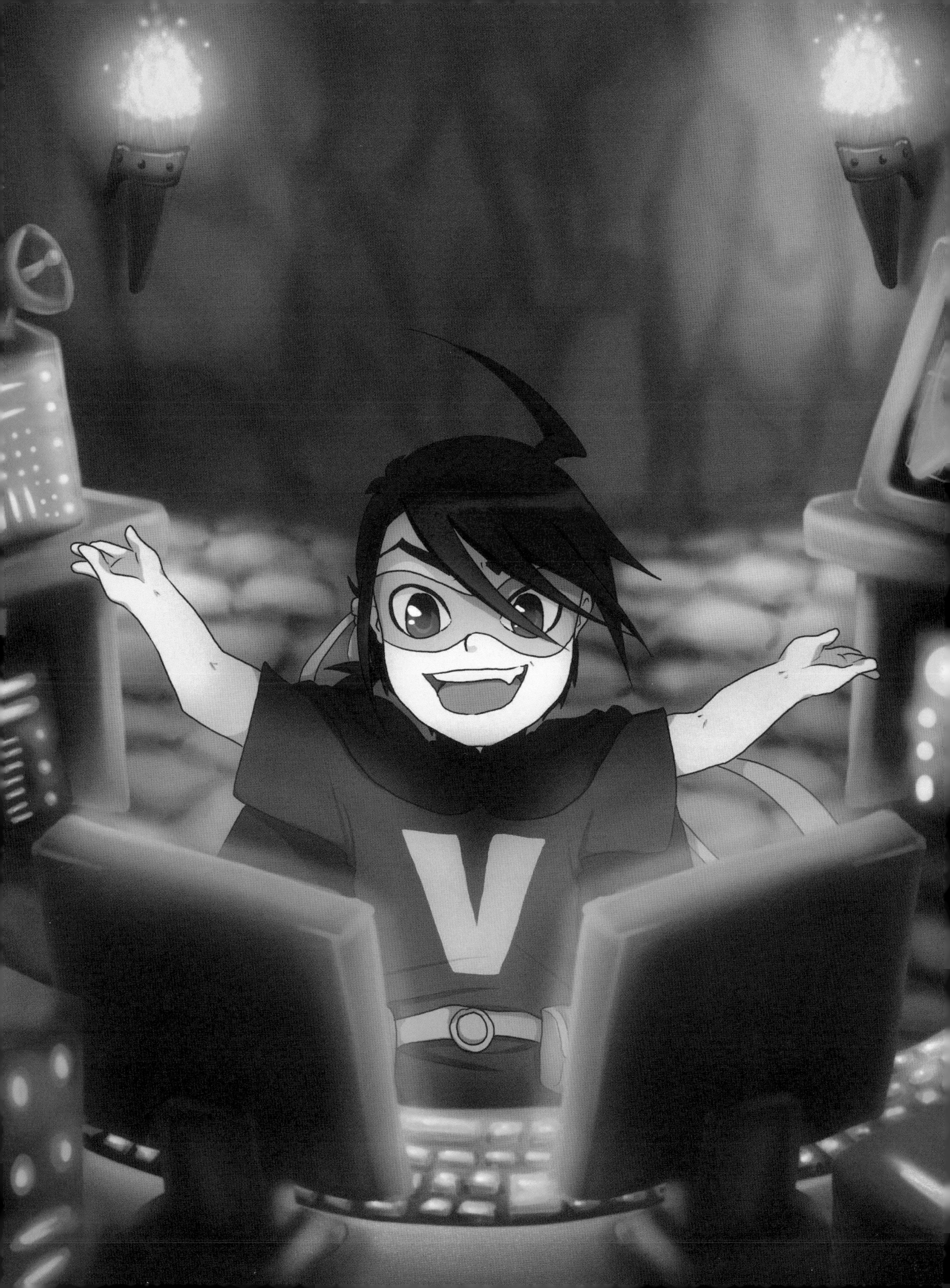

"Next, you have to have a cool evil name. Take mine for instance: Supreme Master of Awesomeness. Now, that's about as cool as you can get, but I'm sure you can come up with something."

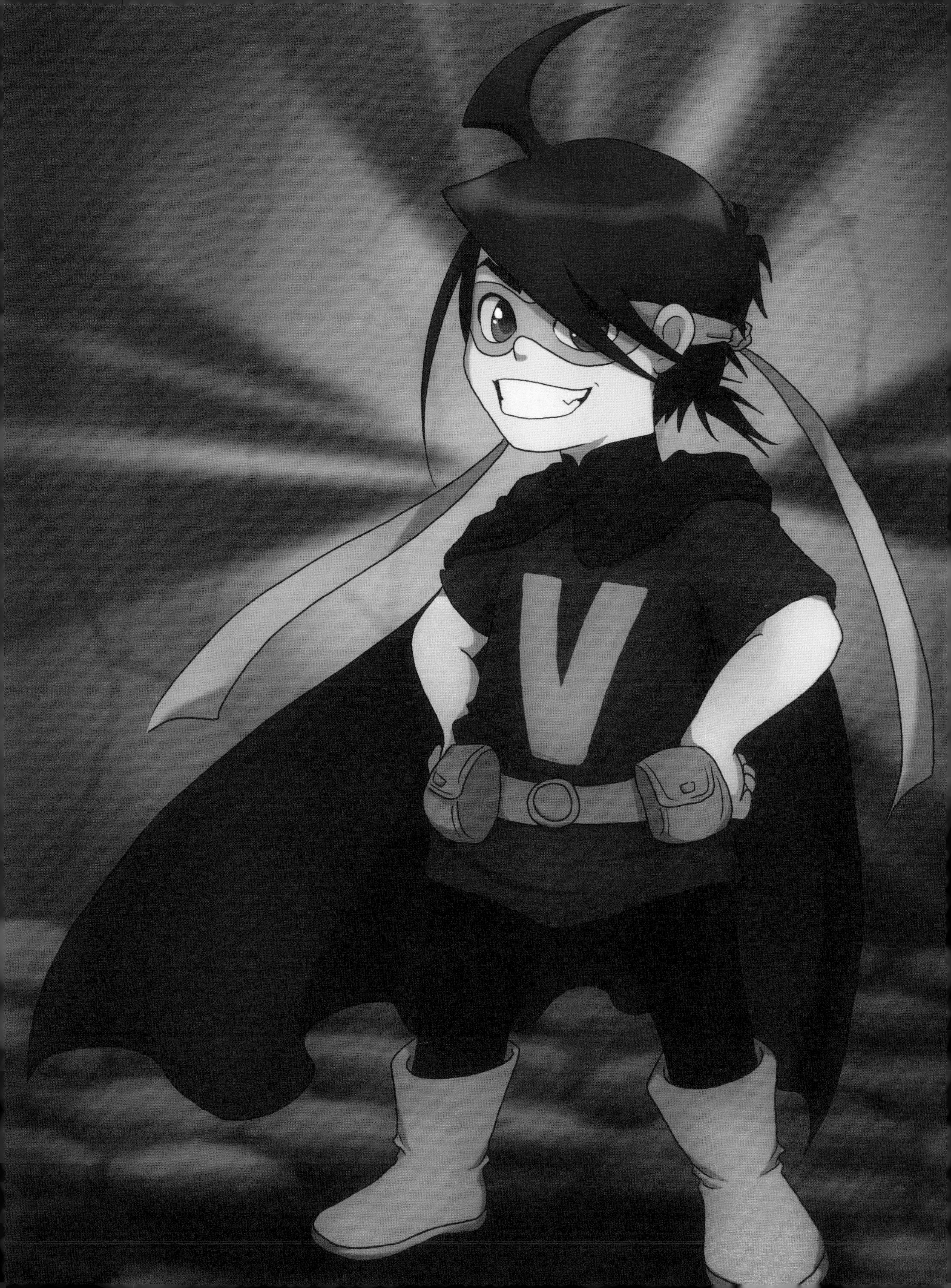

"Third, you need a trendy costume! You'll need all the essential parts: cape, boots, mask, and logo. Also, be sure to have matching pieces! Nobody wants to fight crime in clashing colors. Red, white, and blue seem to be a popular mix."

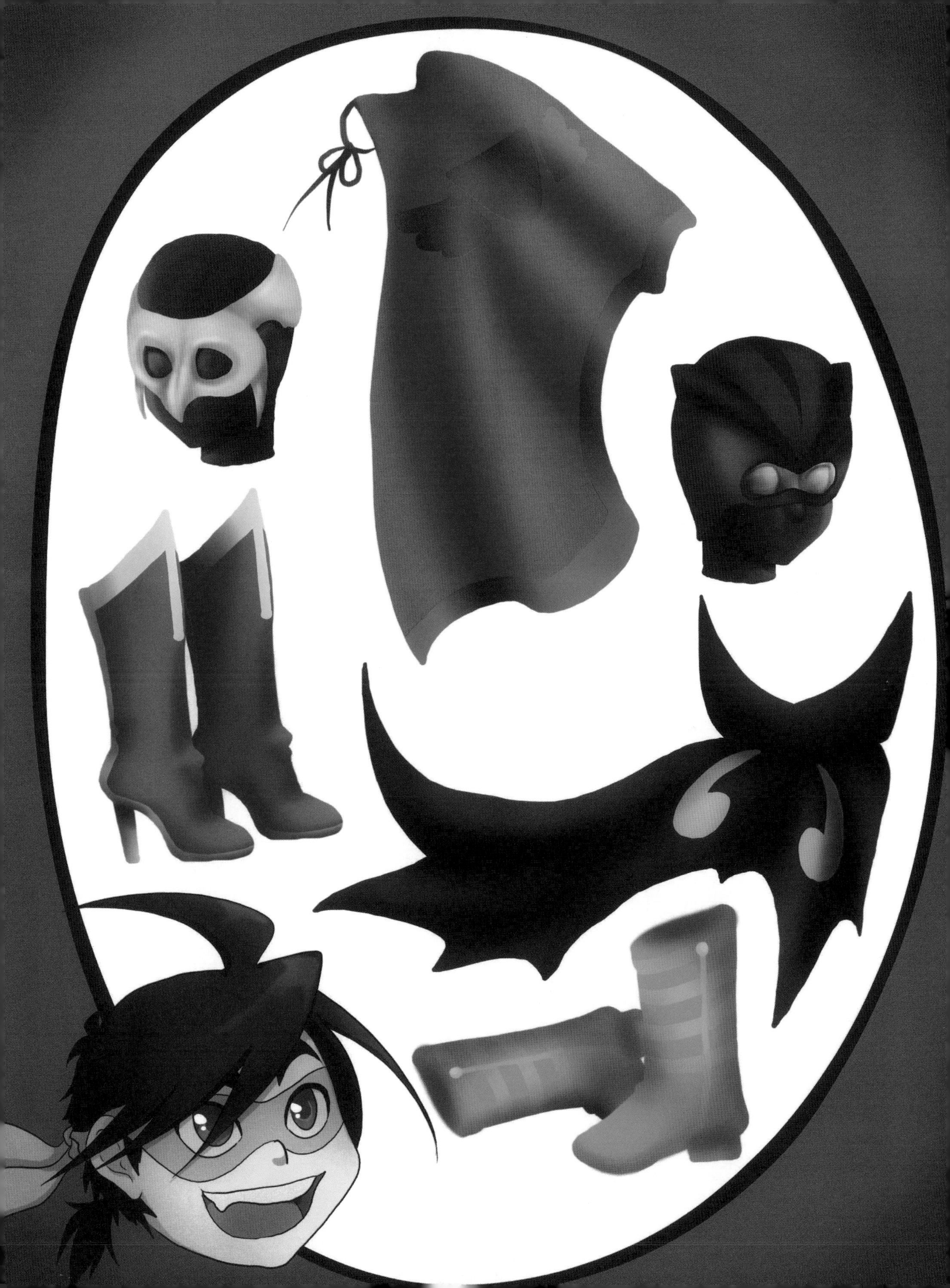

"You'll need to have more than just a lair, a name, and an outfit. You must have an evil laugh. There are many different types. There's the Wicked Cackle, the High-Pitched Screech, the Horrible Wheeze, not to mention the Malevolent Giggle. Why don't you try it with me? Breathe in, then, BWAHAHAHAHAHA! Hear the echo? It pays to have good sound effects in the lair."

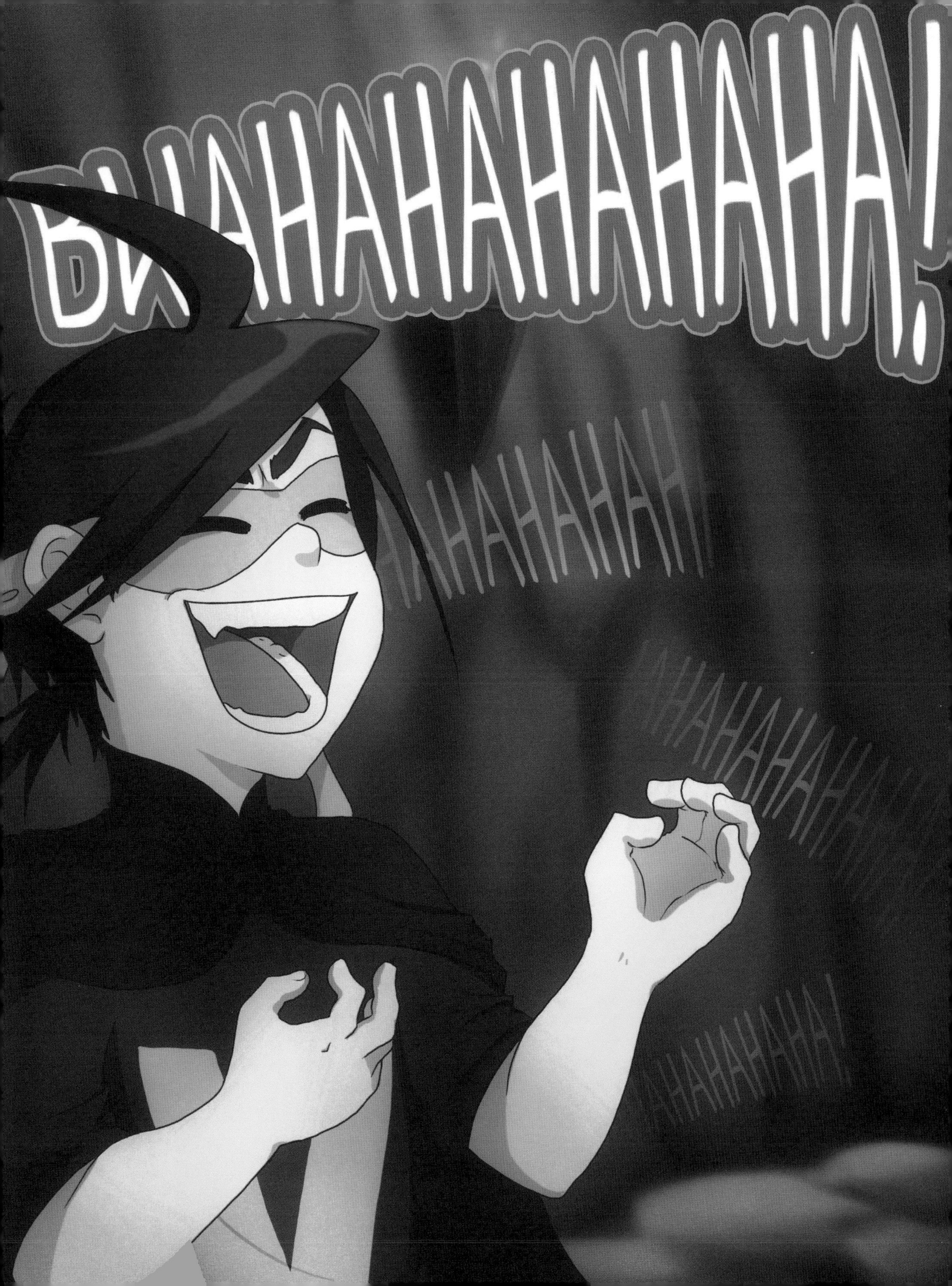
B AHAHAHAHAHAHA!
AHAHAHAHAHAH
AHAHAHAHA
AHAHAHAHA!

"Within the Lair of Awesome, I have several necessary items any Super Villain needs. You've got to have the latest gadgets and gizmos. Also, you'll need a lab to mix chemicals together in order to create EVIL concoctions like prune juice!"

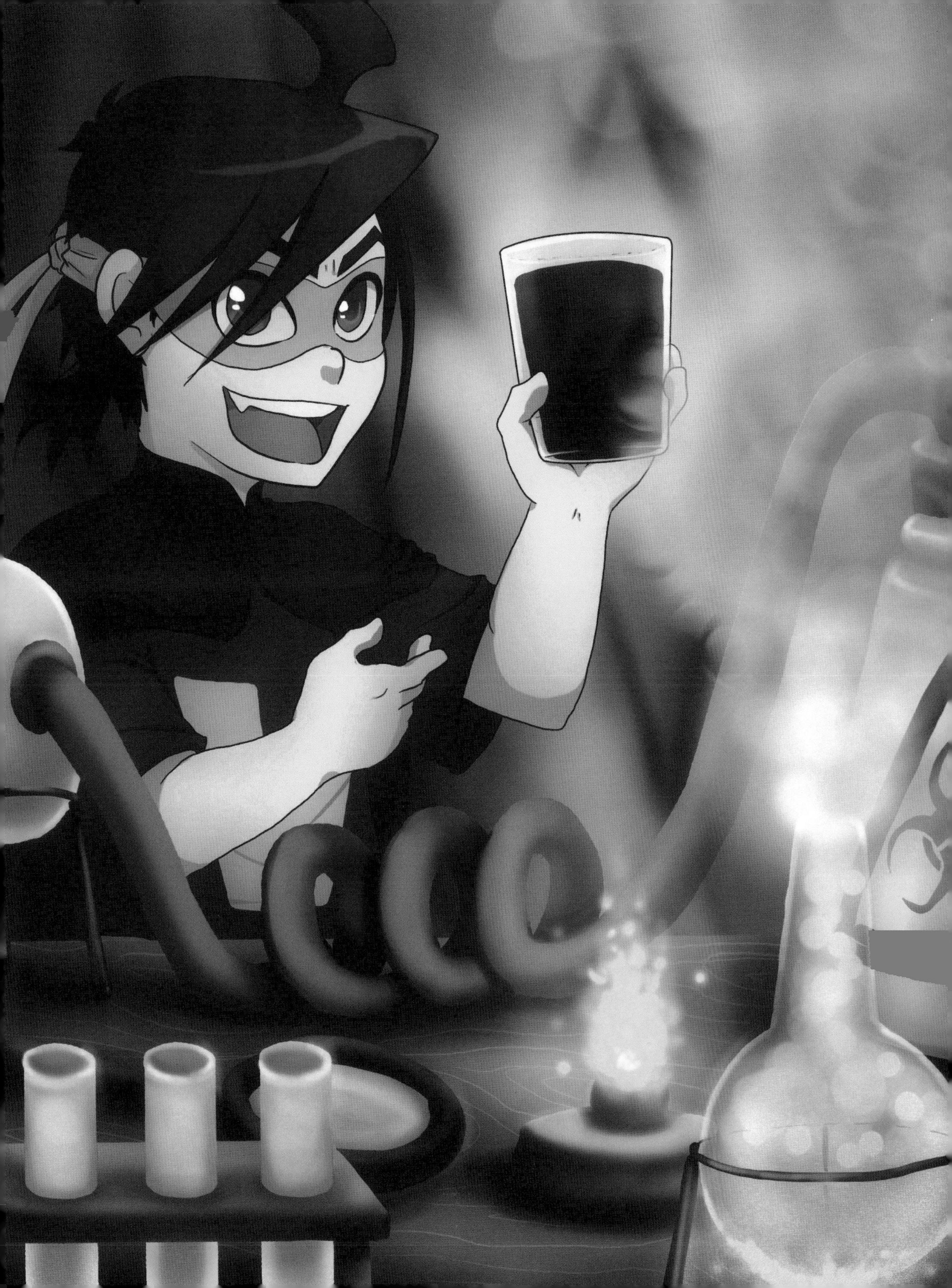

"Although gadgets and gizmos and evil potions are important, there is one thing above all else that a Super Villain has to have: The Chair. The Chair is the throne to the Super Villain, the ultimate seat of power. Not only is it intimidating and a good place to confront dastardly Superheroes, but it can be a nifty place to chill! The Chair here has built in speakers, a hidden compartment for snacks, and a button to open the trapdoor, sending any Heroes into the dungeons!"

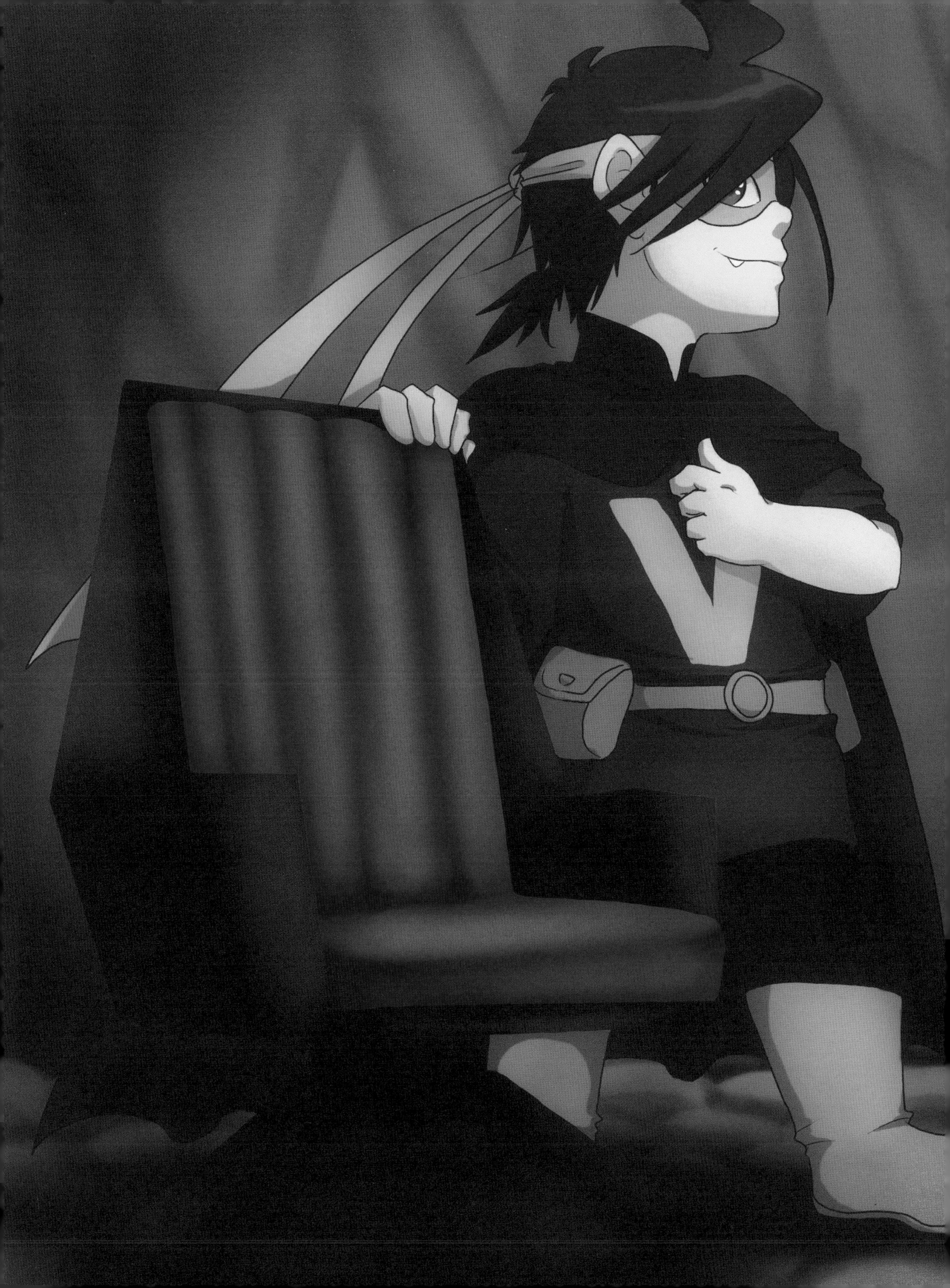

"Let's walk around the Lair of Awesome. As a Super Villain, I have to have the most dangerous—yet most cool—inventions in the world. For instance, take the Big Red Button. Every villain needs one. It is the automatic self-destruct option in all lairs. Very important, but we will not be pushing this one now since we are currently in the Lair. So, I hang this DO NOT PRESS sign here to make sure that no one activates it."

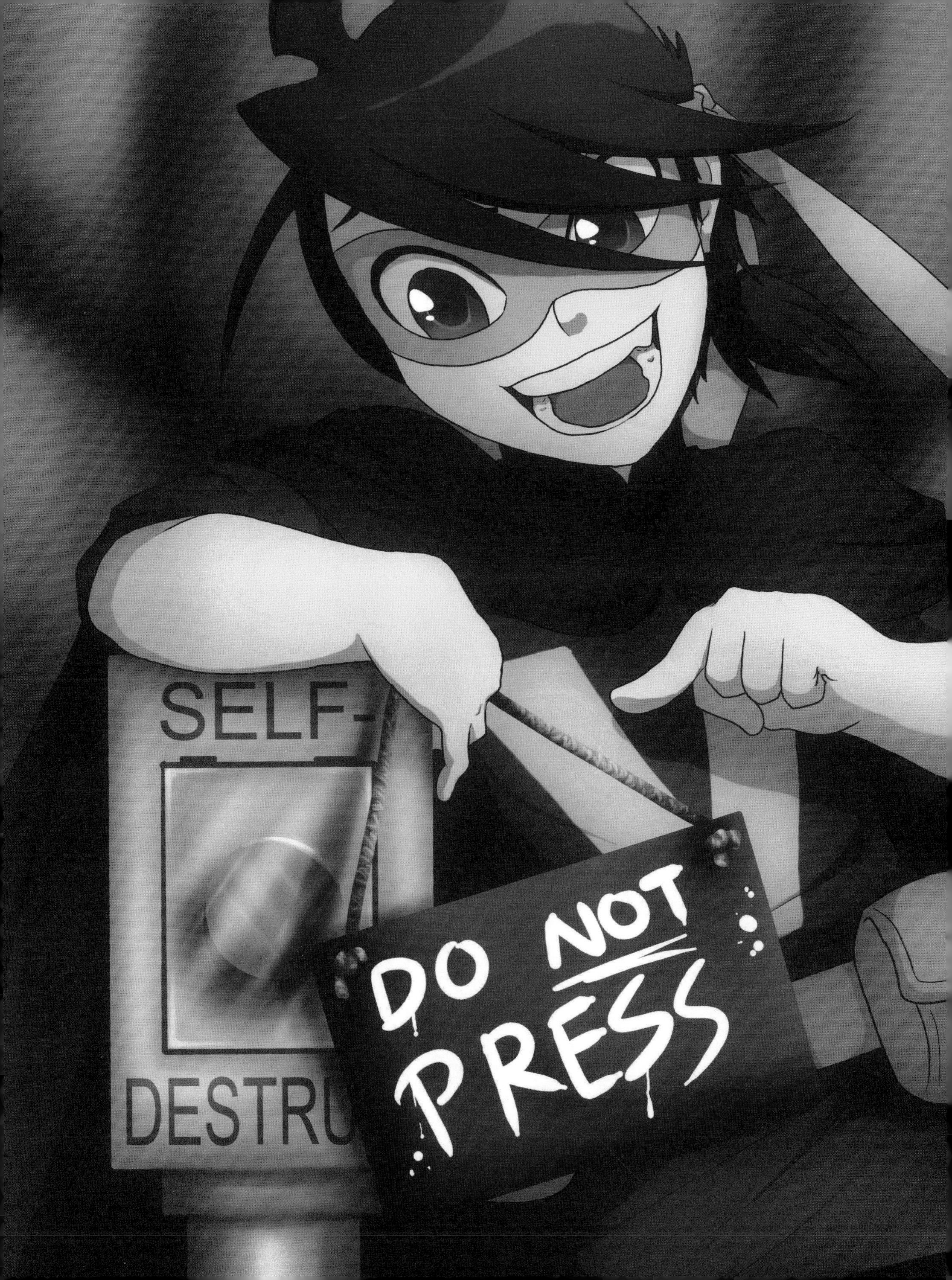
SELF-
DESTRU
DO NOT PRESS

"Of course, someone needs to clean the Lair every once in a while, and as a Super Villain I am too important to stoop to such menial tasks. What you need to do is hire a suitable butler, preferably with an old-fashioned English name like Alcott or Alston. If you can't find a good butler, or if you're the thrifty super villain, you can always just have your mother around like I do. Say, there's my mother now. Mama, look, I'm teaching these people how to be a Super Villain!"

"Humph, I hope they wiped their feet..."

"Just ignore her..."

"He could have been a doctor, or a lawyer. But nooo, he had to be a Super Villain..."

"Let's move on, shall we?"

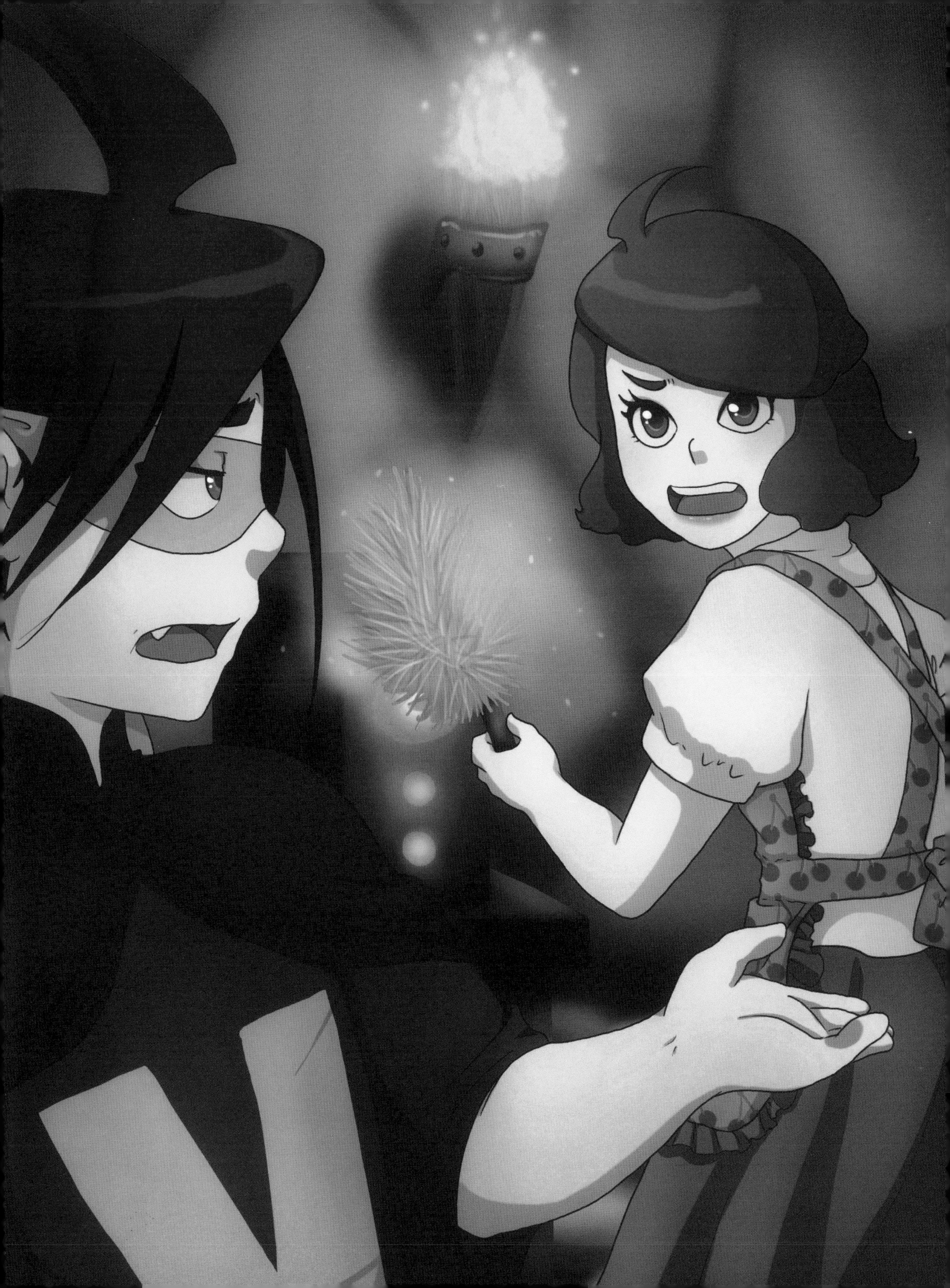

"Being a Super Villain can get lonely. That's why you need henchmen and underlings! They'll carry out your dirty work. Plus, you can get a monster like I have. Meet my one-eyed dog, Buffy. Buffy here is the product of a mad science experiment. She's quite big, but friendly for her size. Watch this.

"Buffy, sit!"

"Woof!"

"Buffy, sit, girl, sit! Ah! Stop licking me!"

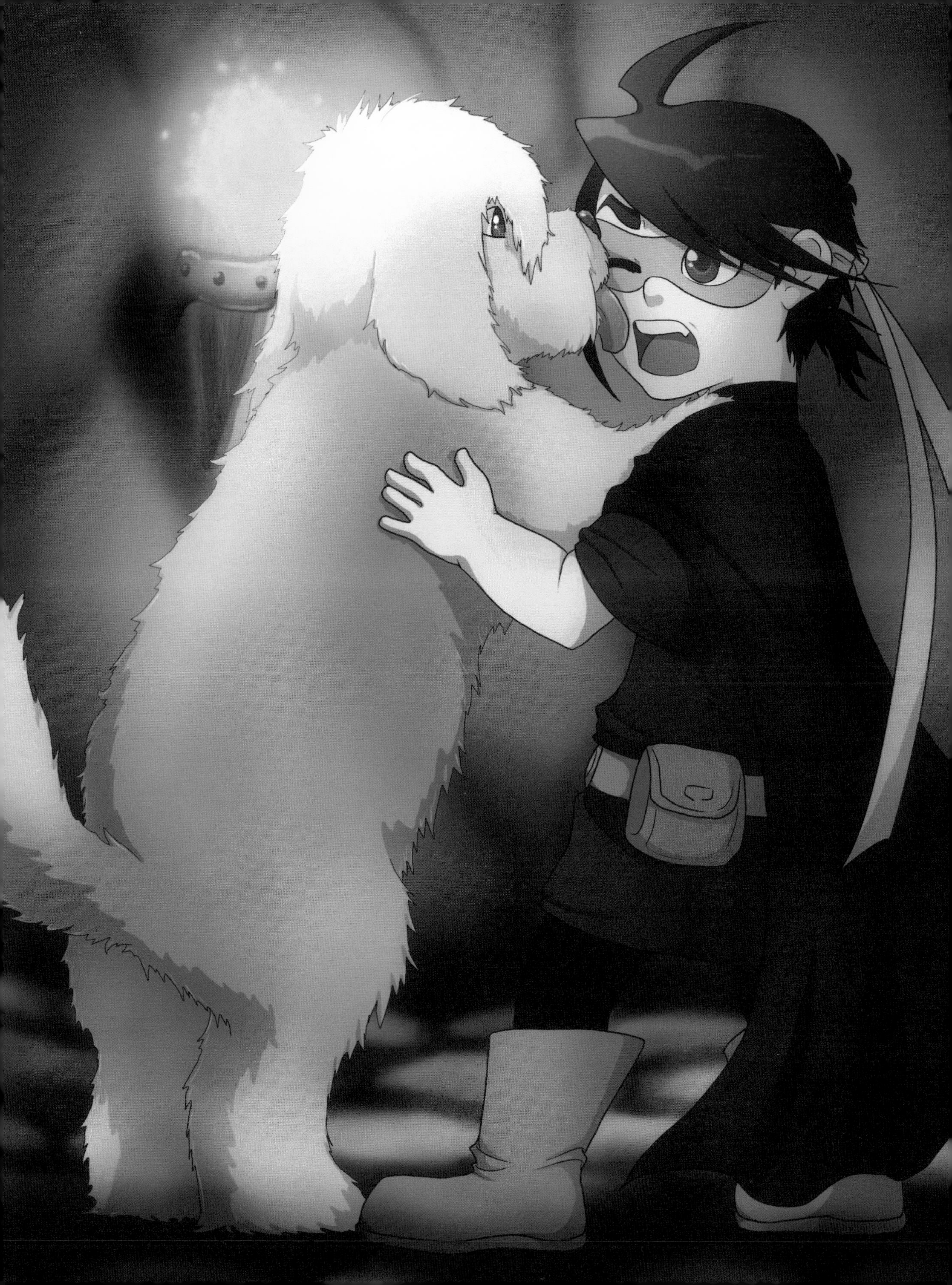

"Around any lair, you have to have good security. Buffy is still in training to be a suitable guard dog, so here at the Lair of Awesome; I have mouse traps, a moat, and a drawbridge. Note the real sea monsters in the moat."

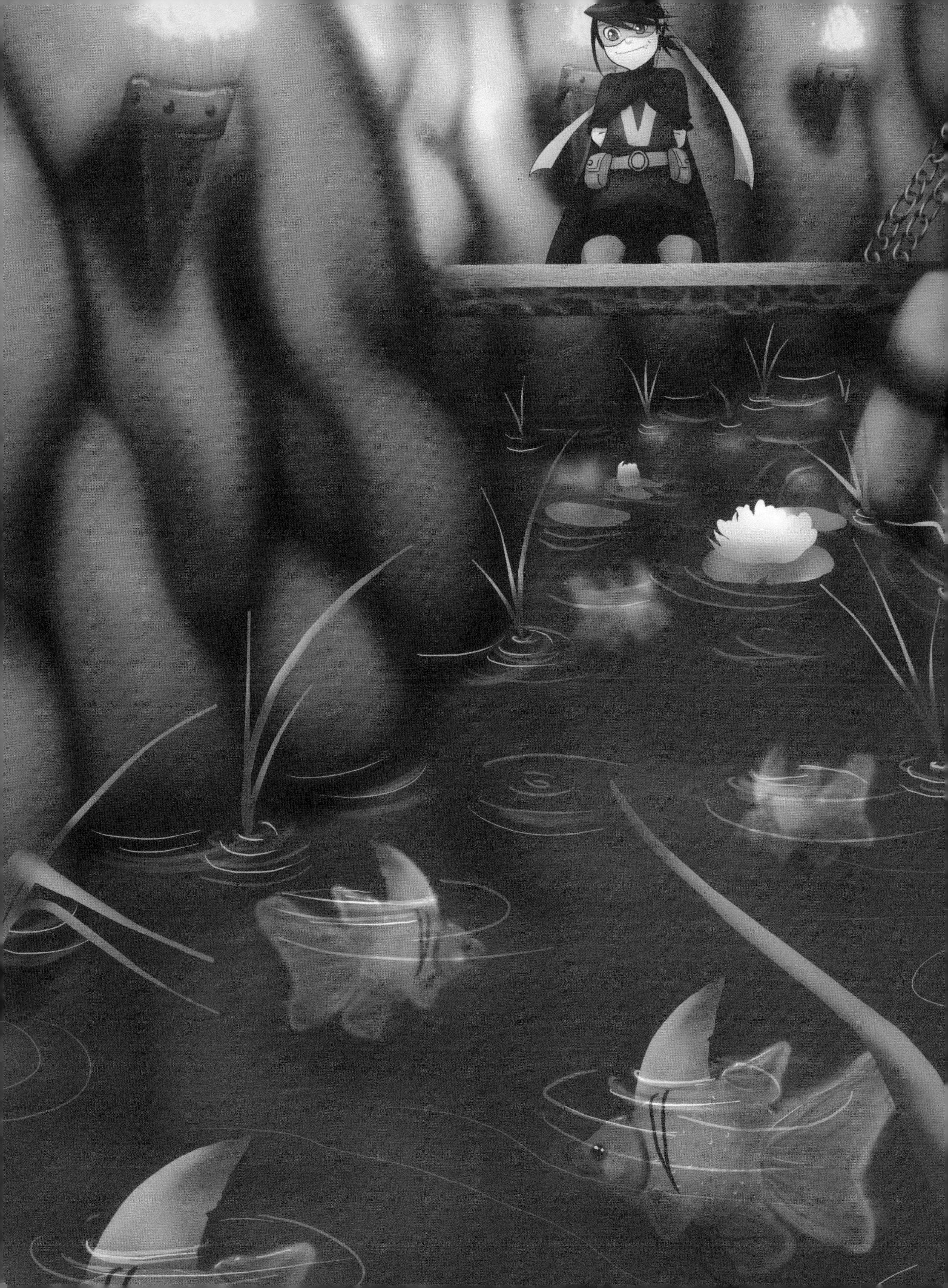

"Now, as a Super Villain, you have to have a Super Computer to do all the thinking for you. Of course, I am a Super Genius, but even Super Geniuses/Super Villains like to kick back sometimes. Meet the Ultimate Computer of Awesomeness! Ultimate Computer of Awesomeness, what is eight plus six?"

"Calculating..."

"This shouldn't take long."

"Calculating..."

"Uh, oh. Oh, well, we'll just be patient...and wait...and wait...and wait...and wait..."

"Calculating complete."

"At last! My Ultimate Computer of Awesomeness is done calculating! Ultimate Computer of Awesomeness, what is the answer?"

"Eight plus six equals two hundred and forty-three."

"...it still has some kinks to work out."

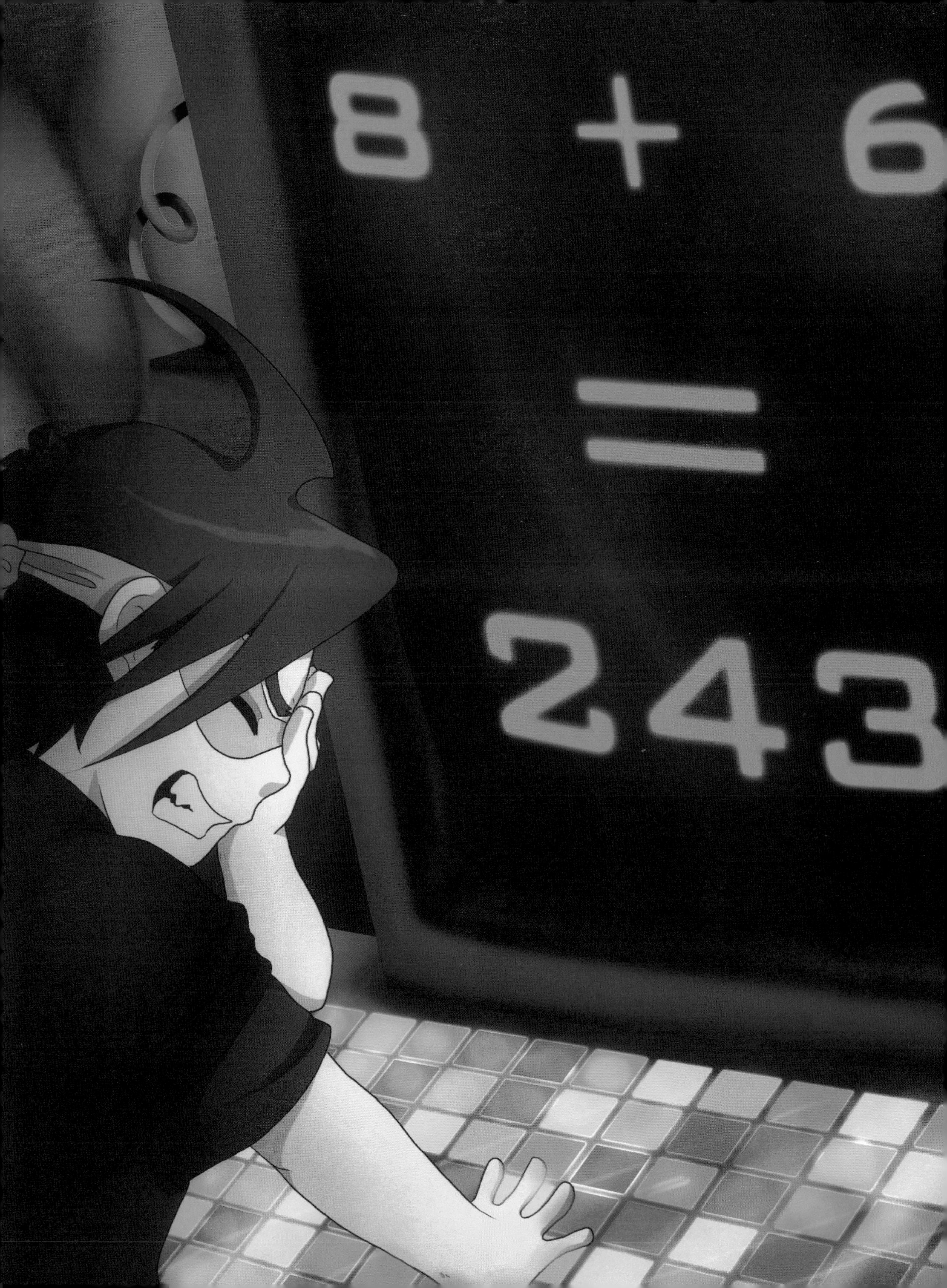
8 + 6
=
243

"Listen, as Supreme Master of Awesomeness, I'm pretty powerful, not to mention *awesome*. But like all Super Villains and Heroes, I've got a—*cough*—a secret weakness. There are many things that can be a secret weakness, such as Kryptonite, sunshine, money, and garlic. What is my secret weakness, you might ask? Well, I'm not telling you!"

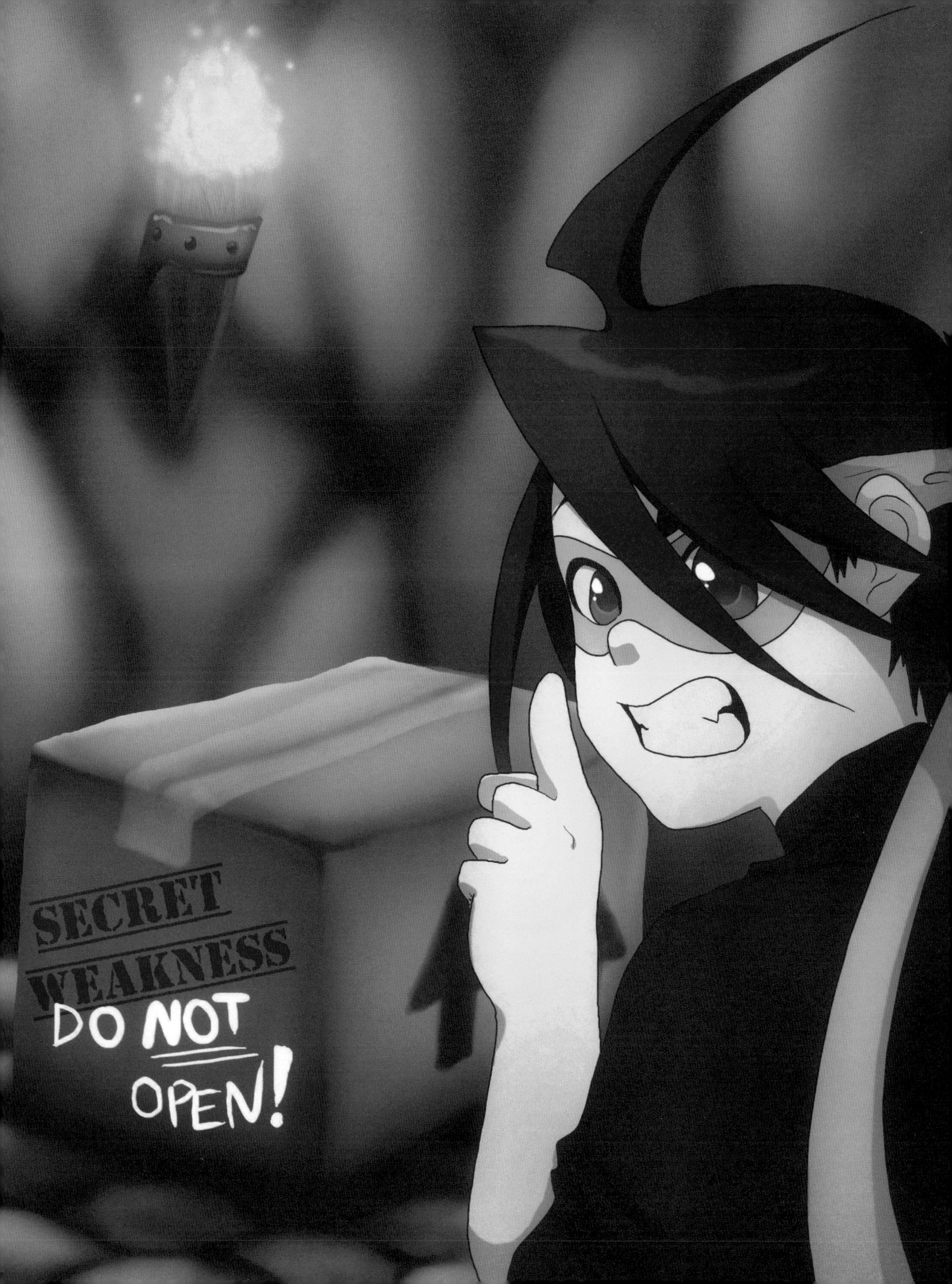
SECRET
WEAKNESS
DO NOT
OPEN!

"There is one final, extremely important thing that all Super Villains must—absolutely *must*—have. And that is a Superhero. Superheroes are annoying, pesky little do-gooders. But everyone needs to have an archenemy. Otherwise, who would we fight? Who would we defeat? Who would we gloat over? That is the only reason Superheroes are still around: to give us Super Villains amusement."

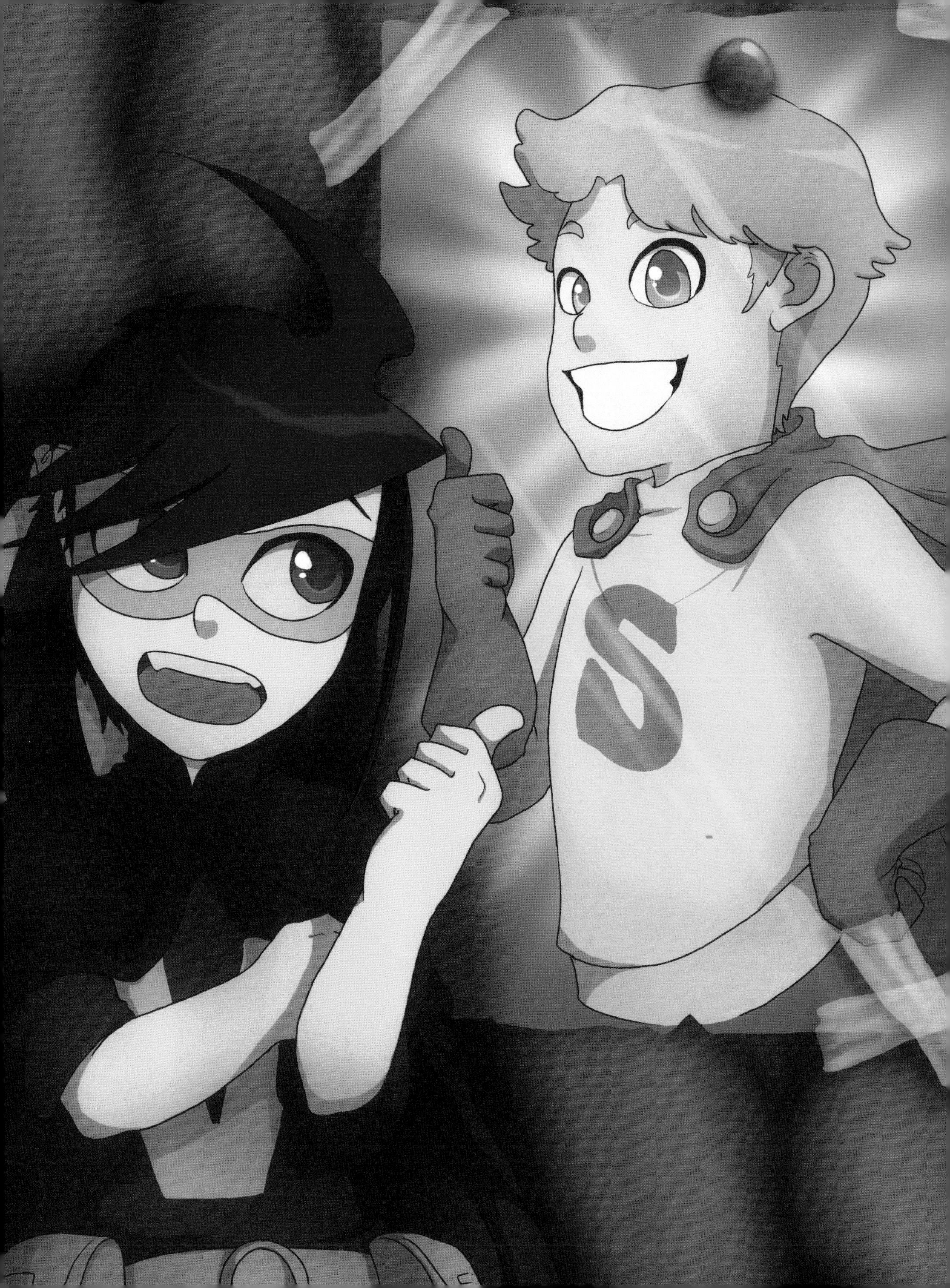

"What, exactly, is a Superhero? They are Boy Scout goody two-shoes! Oh, sure, they get all the cool cars and fan clubs, but really they're just for show. All they care about is their bronze statues sitting in City Hall. I mean, anyone can get a cat out of a tree or help an old lady cross the street. It takes true genius to conquer the world!"

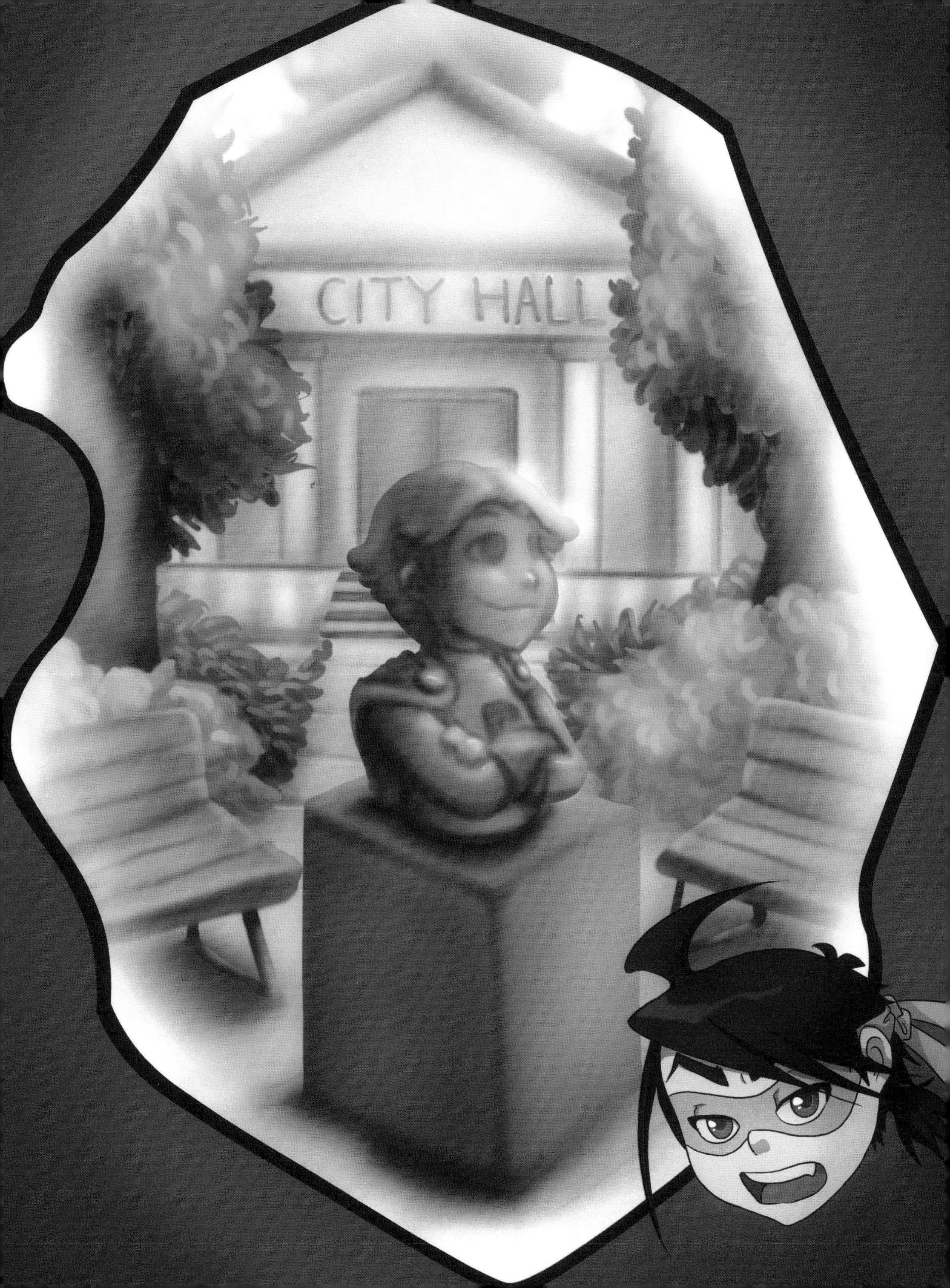
CITY HALL

"Unfortunately, Superheroes are a jealous type and don't like sharing the limelight, which is why they always get in the way when a true genius like me *tries* to conquer the world. You can recognize a superhero by their long speeches of good and truth and justice and all that other trash. They're also notorious front-page hoggers."

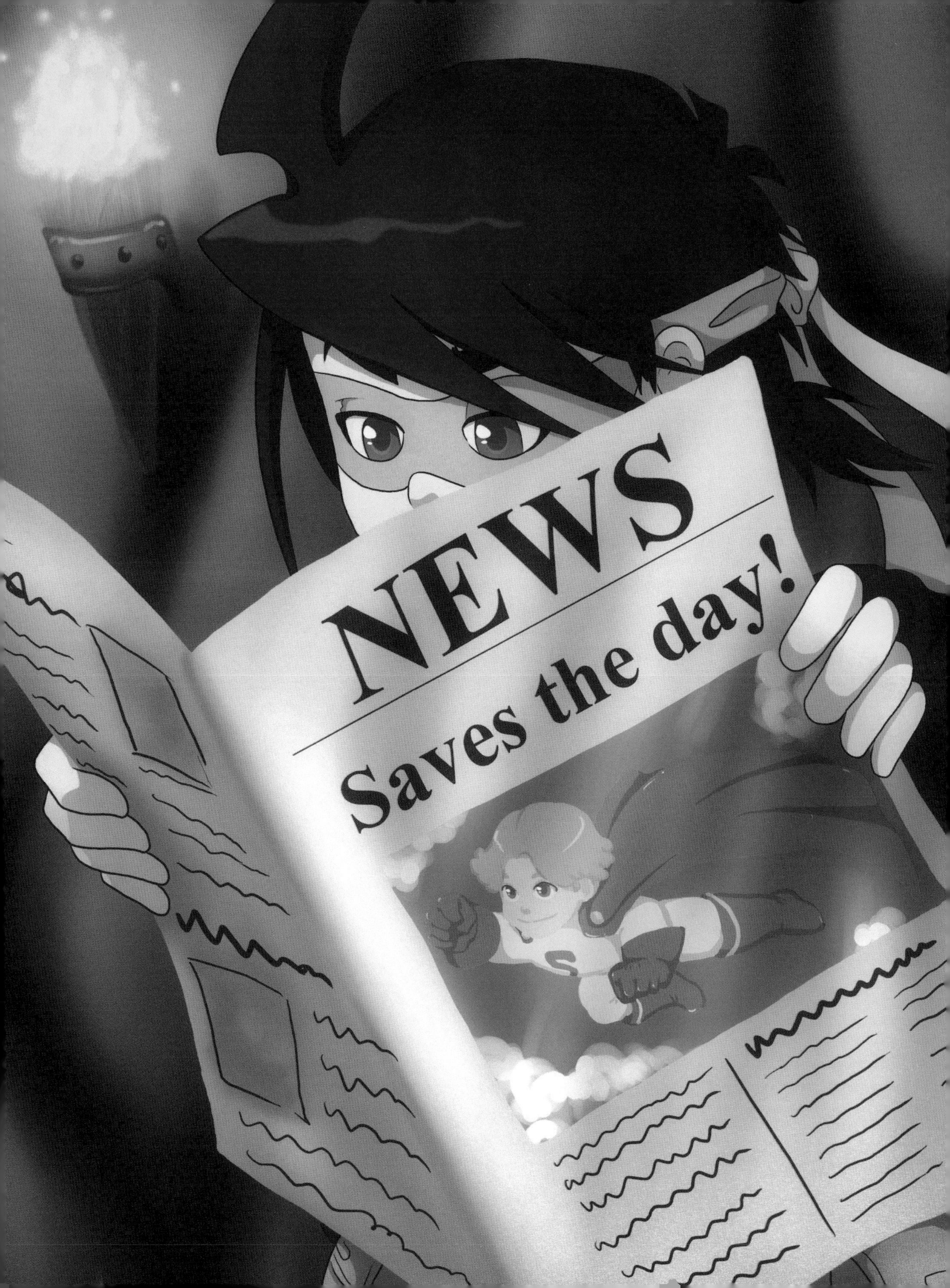
NEWS
Saves the day!

"Now, to defeat a Superhero, you have to come up with an elaborate plan full of details and tidbits of facts. This is why I have a chalkboard! I also have five different colors of chalk."

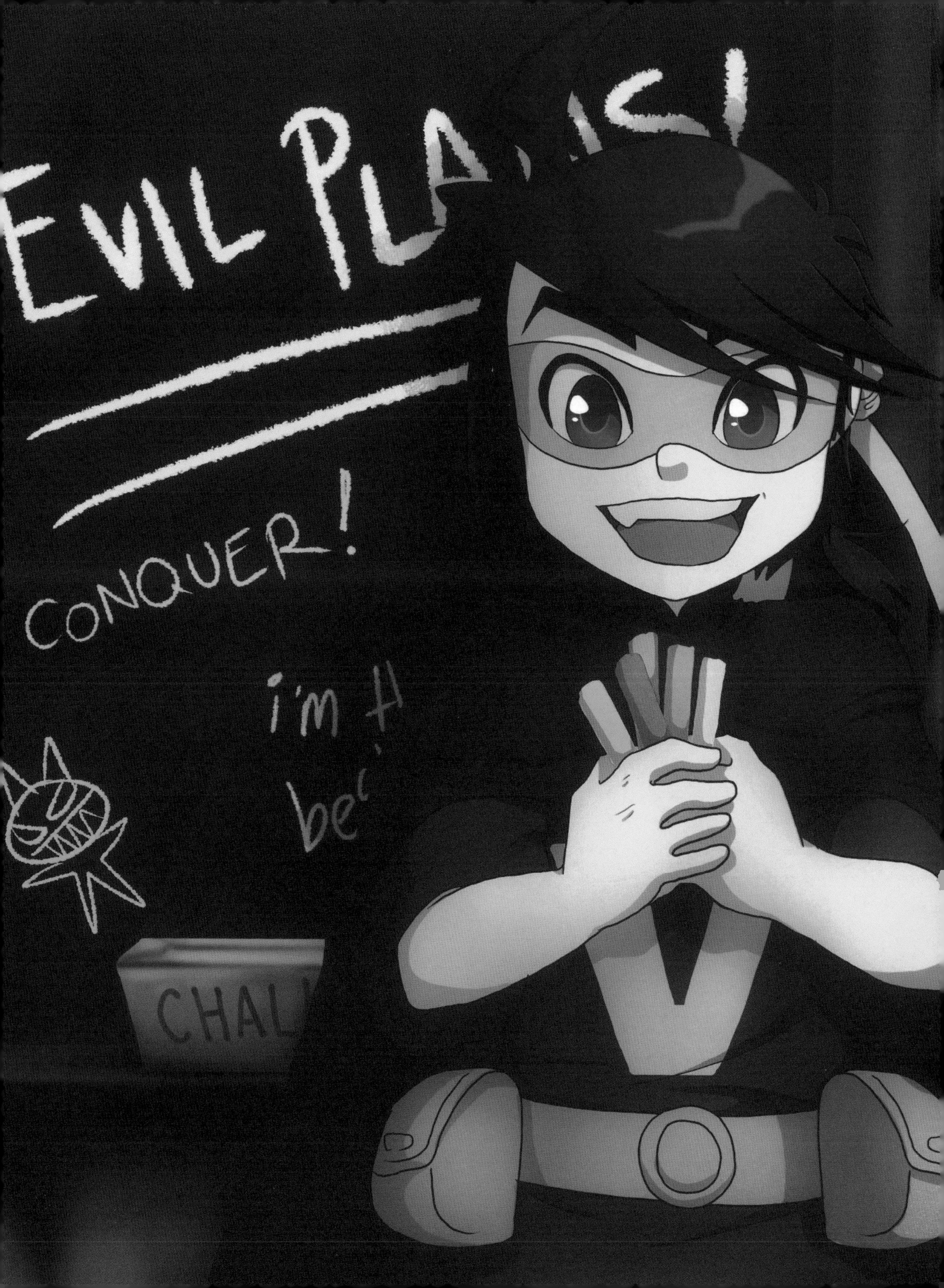
EVIL PLA
CONQUER!
i'm t
be
CHAL

"A Super Villain's Master Plan is usually something along the lines of world domination. Examples are creating an army of robot cats, blocking out the sun, turning the moon into cheese, etc. You may want to start off a bit smaller at first and build your way up."

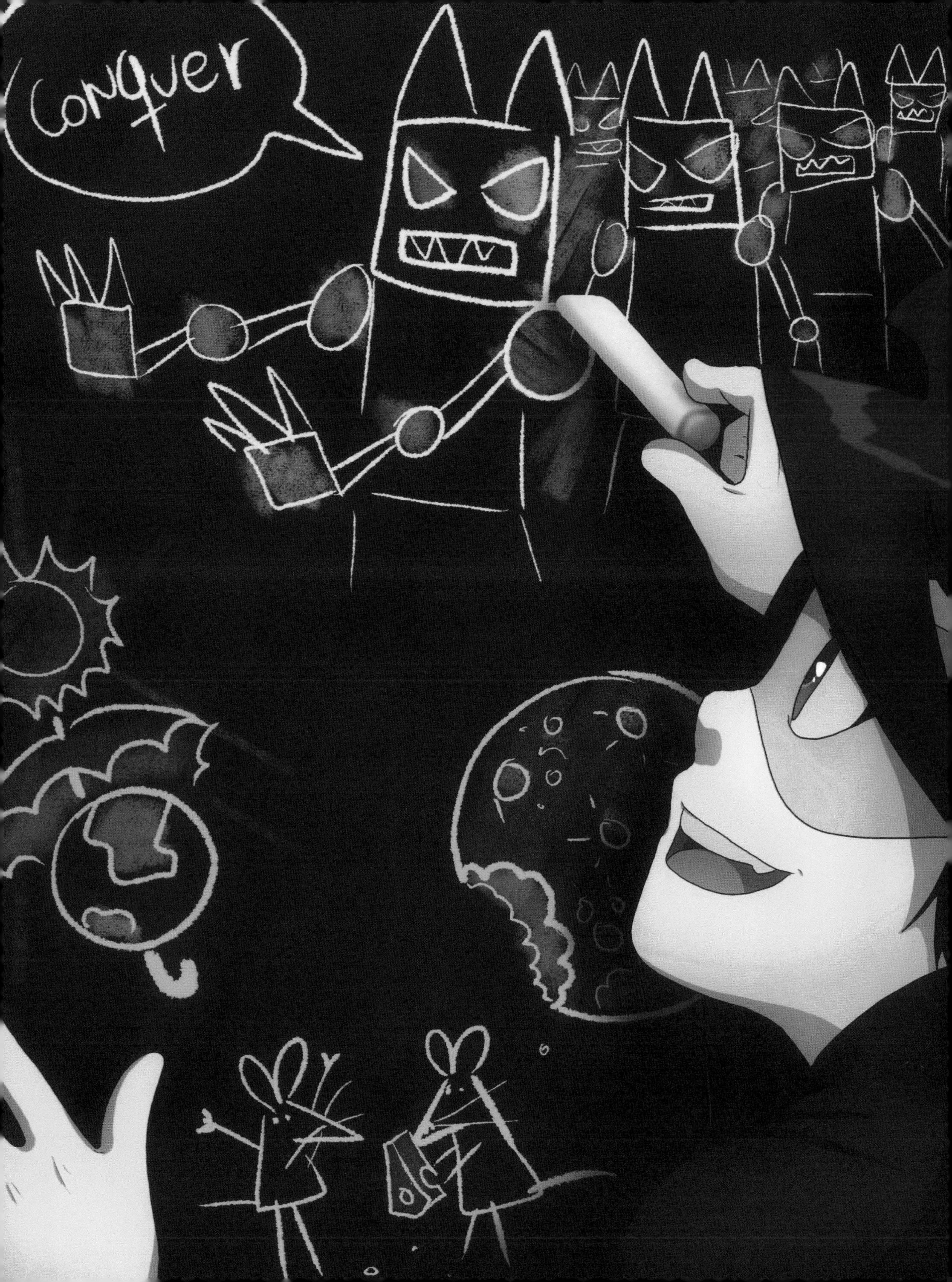
Conquer

"Once you have your Master Plan down, you need to come up with a brilliant victory speech which you shall give once you have captured your Superhero. You'll need to address all the essential points: why you became a Super Villain, why you dislike Superheroes, why you dislike them in particular, what is your whole evil plan, how you will takeover the city/country/world, et cetera, etc. You should include a good catch phrase as well, something like *you thought you had seen the last of me, eh?*"

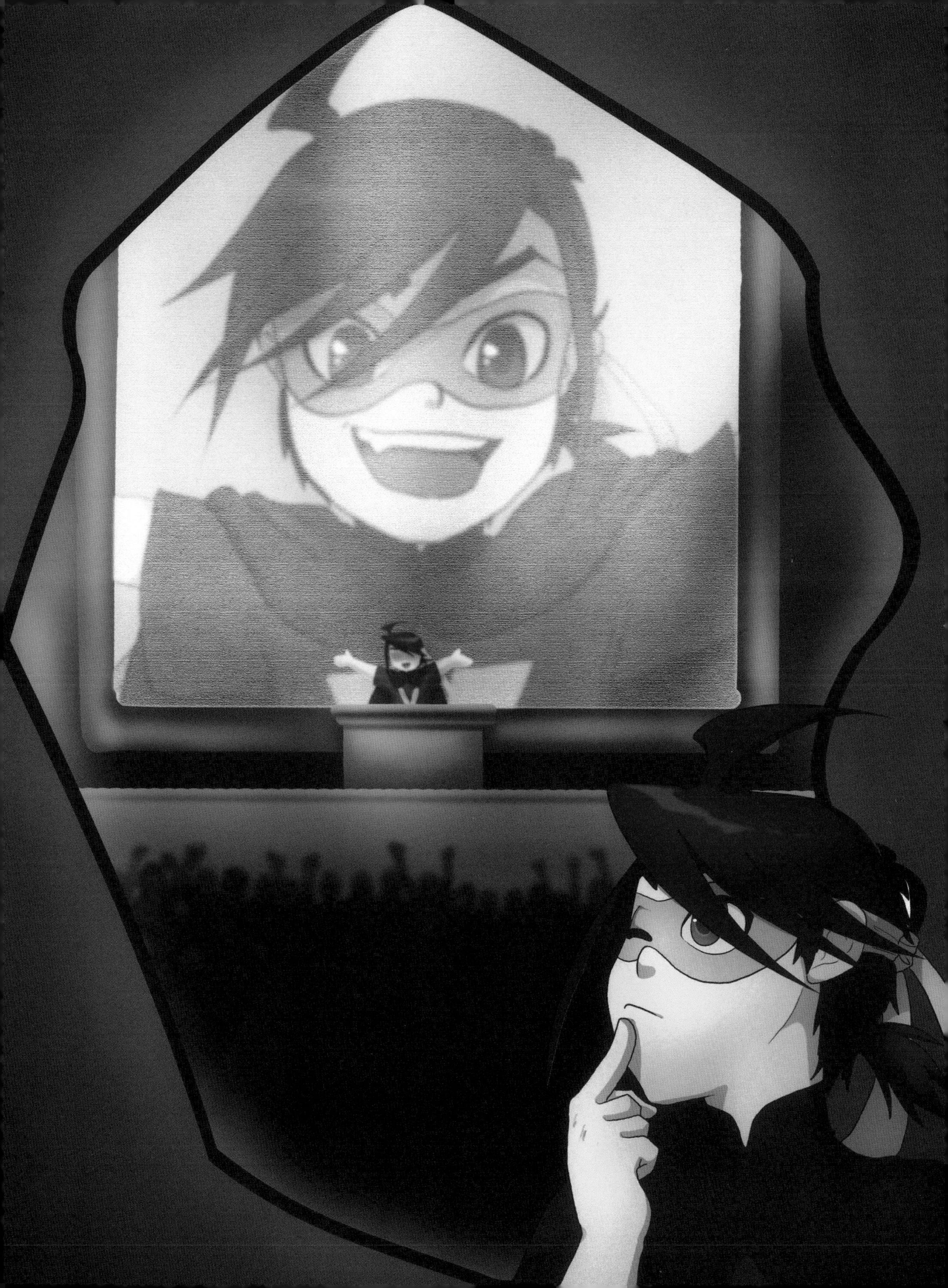

"Well, so long! I am off to conquer the world! I shall defeat my archenemy, Superior Guy! What a ridiculous name that is, right? Anyway, I should be back later with the world at my feet."

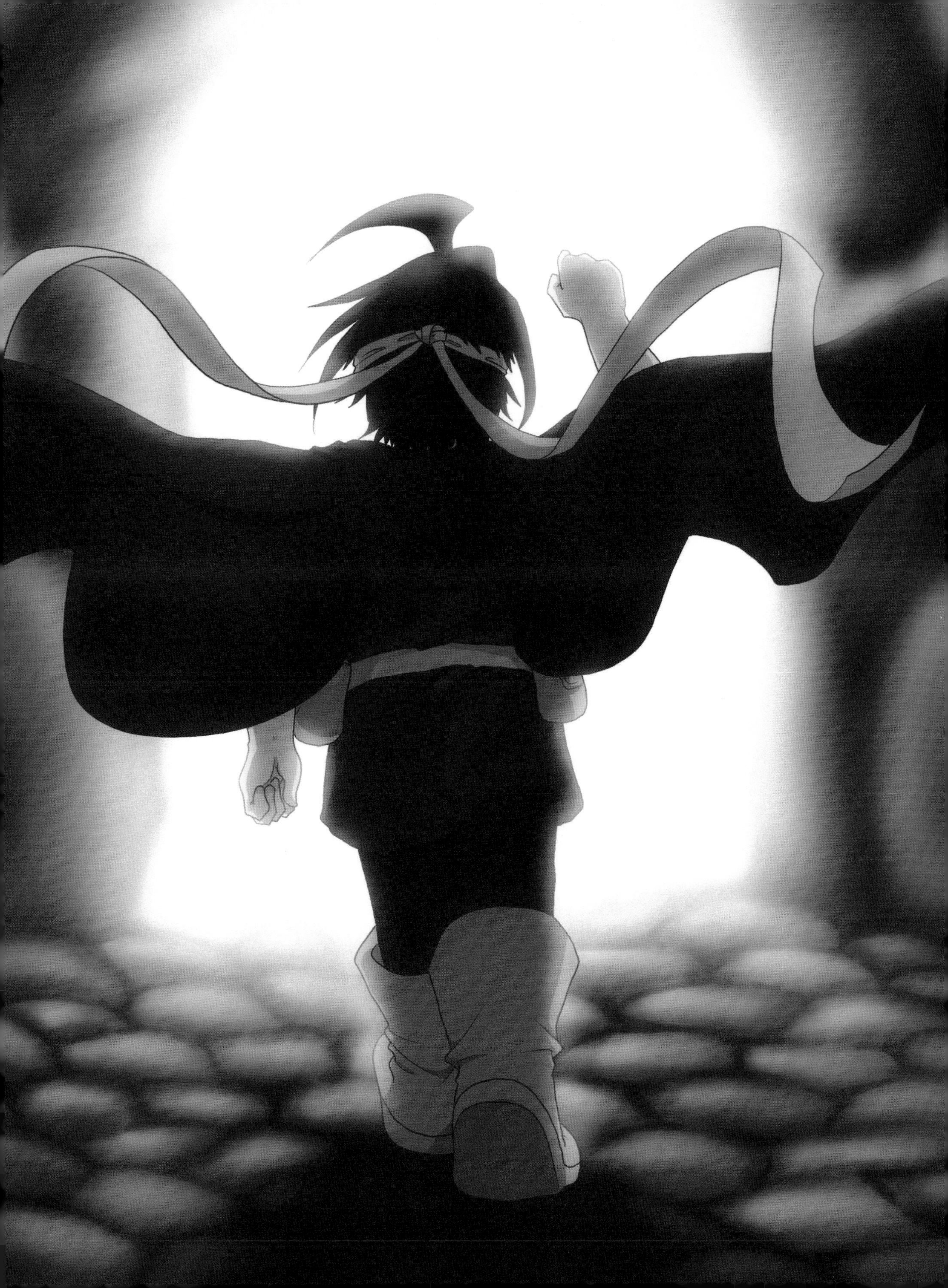

Super-Duper-Opolis City Prison

"Note, this may be a snag for some of your schemes."

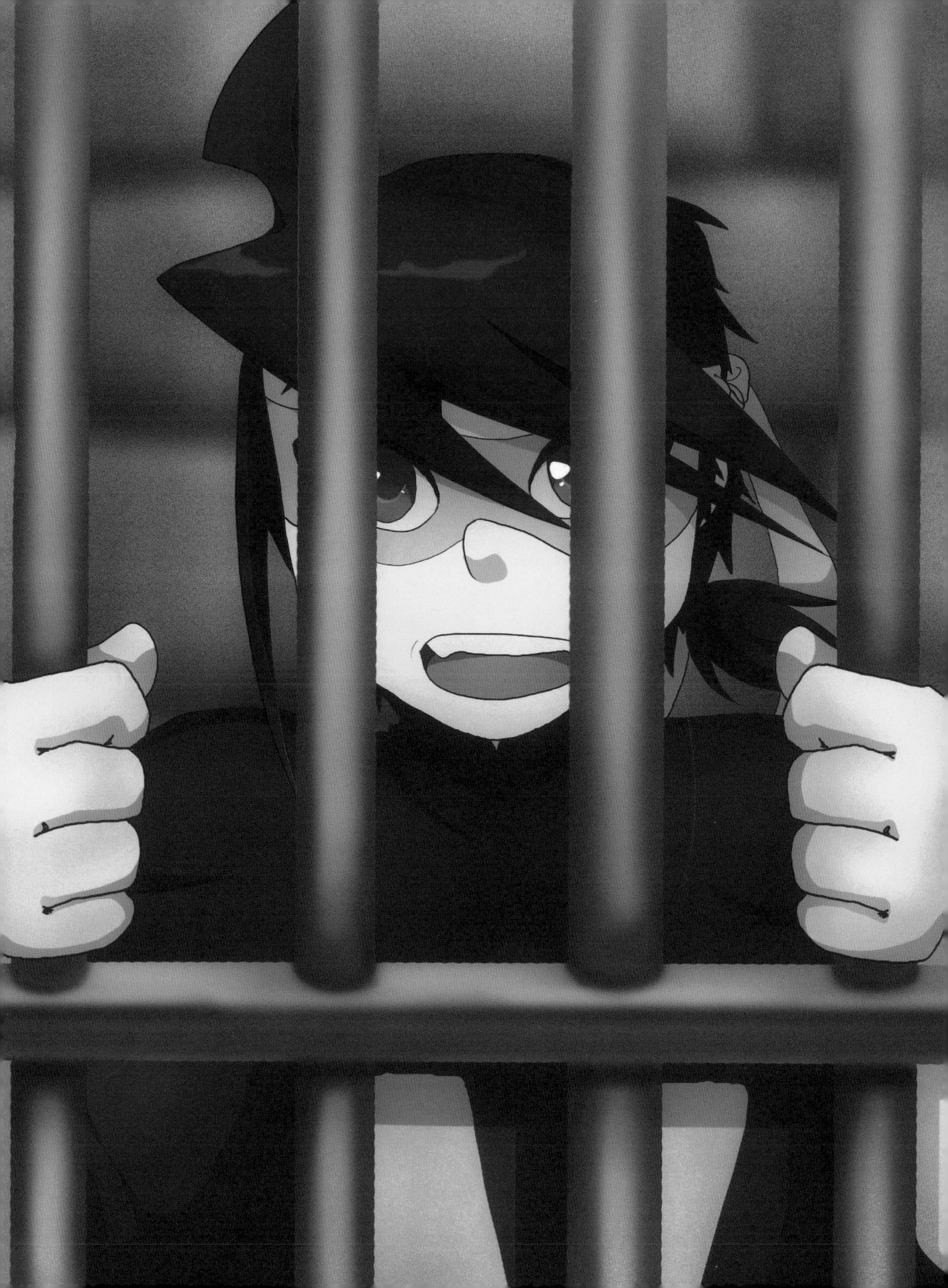

"But never fear! Every Super Villain has a fallback escape plan. For the amateur, you may have to conduct this plan quite often."

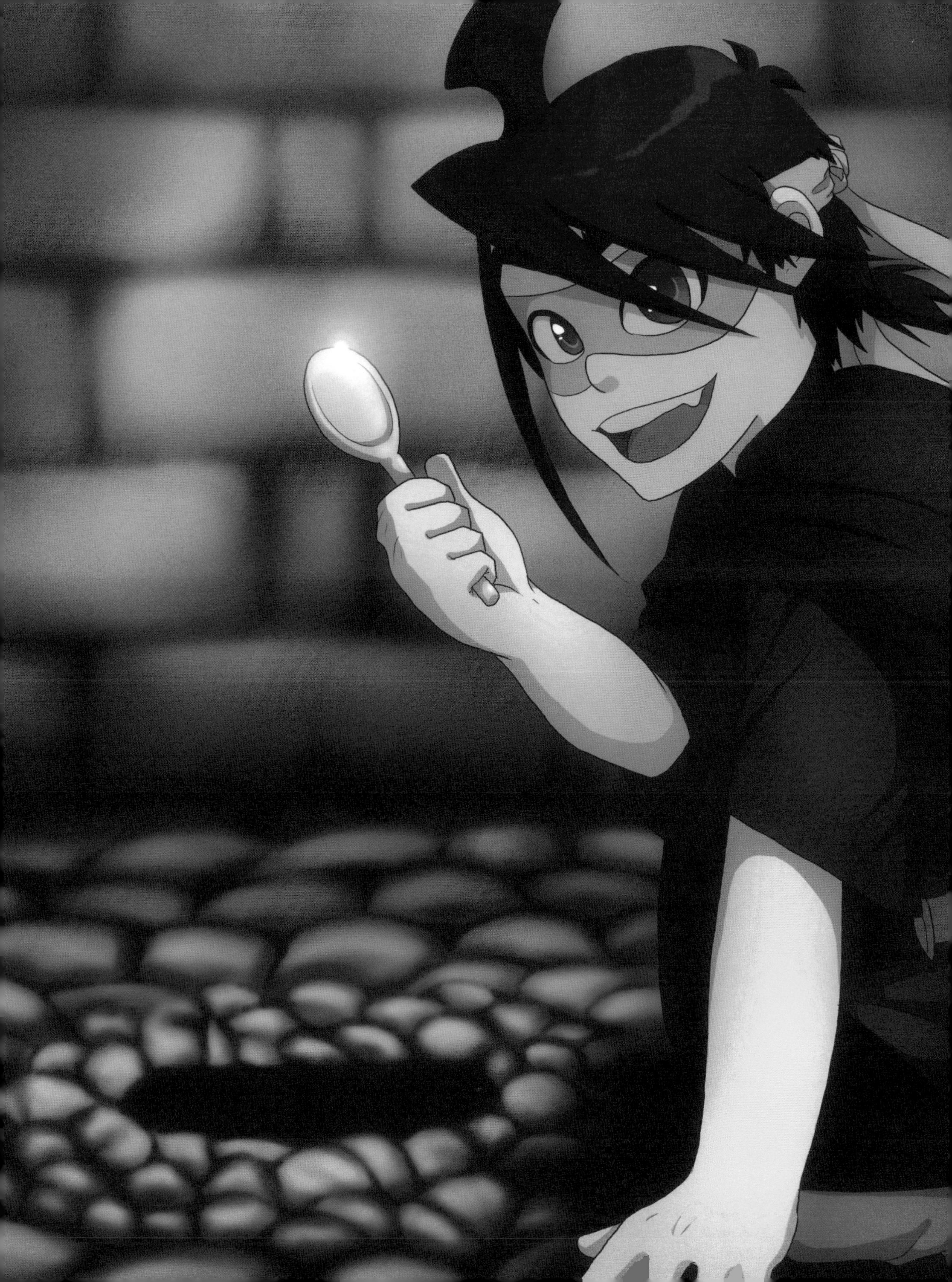

"No prison can hold the Supreme Master of Awesomeness! There, I have escaped! Quick, back to the Lair of Awesome!"

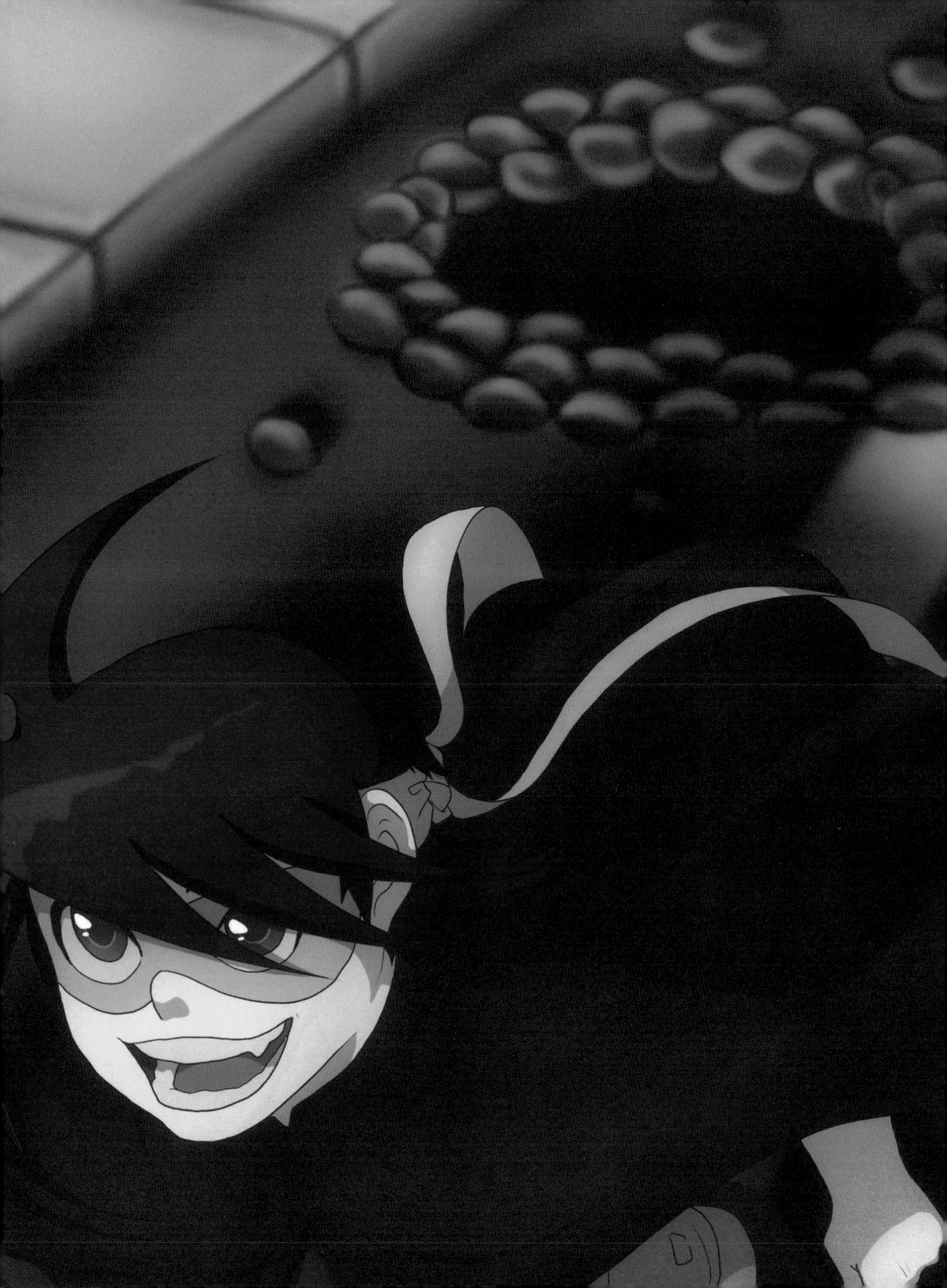

"I know what you're thinking, and I KNOW. My first plan might have failed, and Superior Guy may have won, but that does not mean the Supreme Master of Awesomeness gives up! A Super Villain never gives up! And when I say never, I mean NEVER!"

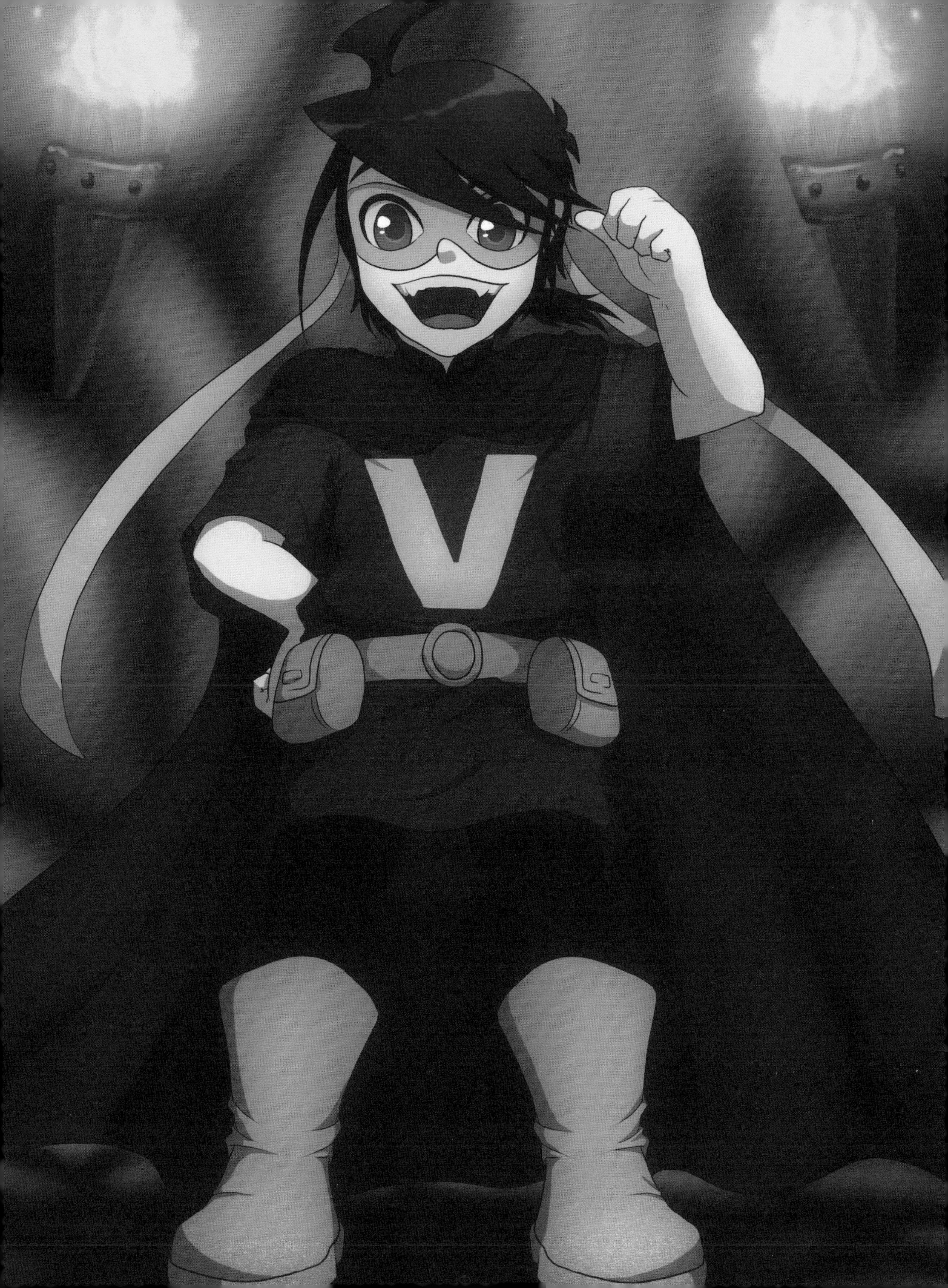

"Well, it's back to the ol'chalkboard for me…"

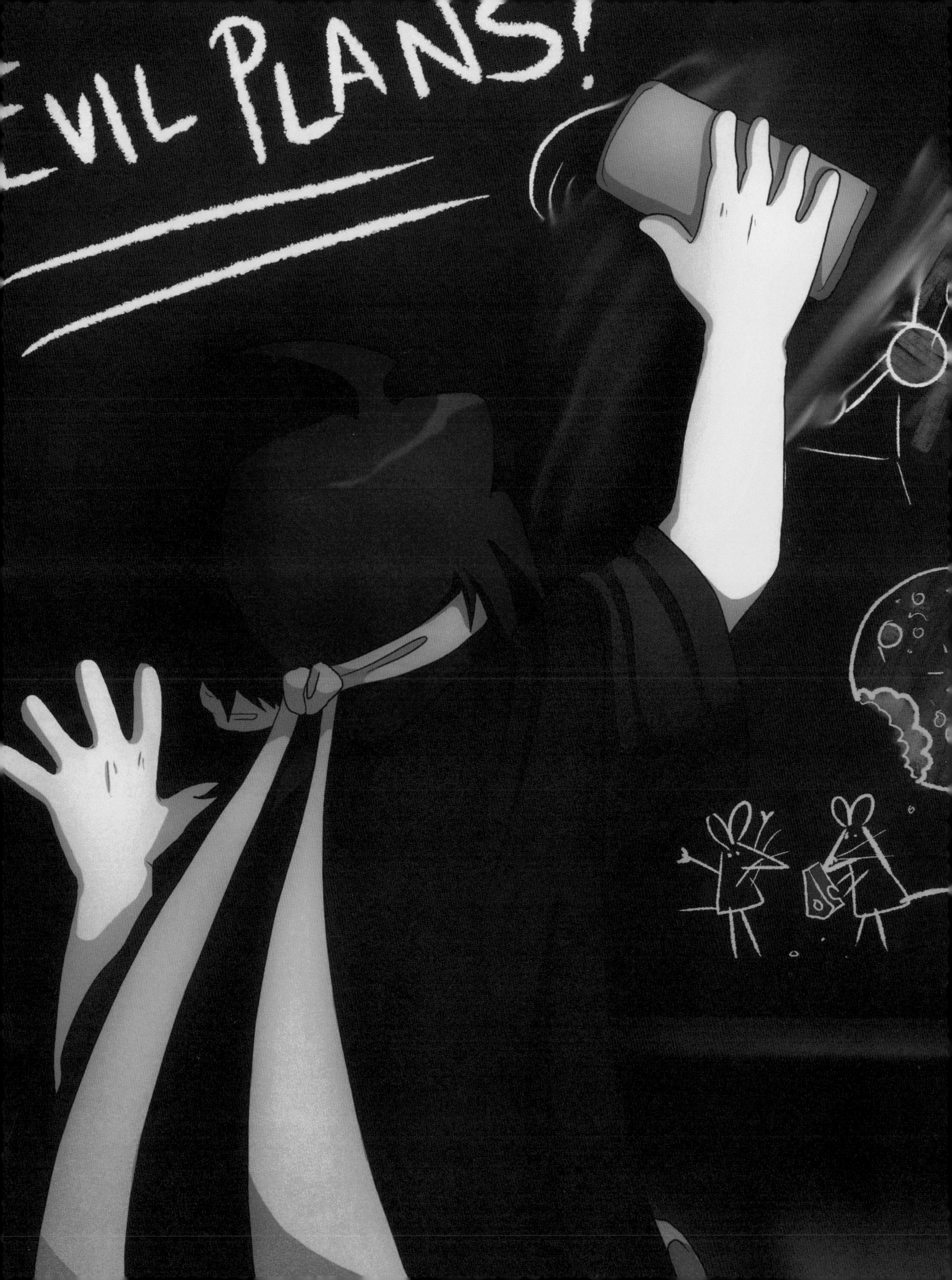
EVIL PLANS!

13326992R30032

Made in the USA
San Bernardino, CA
21 July 2014